Welcome to the

Bagpuss

ANNUAL
2001

£5.99
UK only

Contents

Original stories written by Oliver Postgate
Scripts adapted by Davey Moore
Illustrated by Peter Firmin and Nick Spender of Advocate
Owl of Athens appliqué by Joan Firmin
Designed by Jeannette Slater and edited by Stephanie Sloan

Screen grabs supplied by GBM Advertising Additional photographs by David Spinner courtesy of Lightweight Designs
Published in Great Britain in 2000 by Egmont World Limited, a division of Egmont Holding Limited,
Deanway Technology Centre, Wilmslow Road, Handforth, Cheshire SK9 3FB
Printed in Italy ISBN 0 7498 4873 1

Once upon a time, not so long ago, there was a little girl and her name was Emily ...
... and she had a shop.

There it is.
It was rather an unusual shop because it didn't sell anything.

You see, everything in that shop window was a thing that somebody had once lost and Emily had found, and brought home to Bagpuss,

Emily's cat Bagpuss ...

the most
important ...

the most
beautiful ...

the most
magical ...

... saggy old cloth cat in the whole wide world.

Well now. One day, Emily found a thing.

She brought it back to the shop and put it down in front of Bagpuss who was in the shop window, fast asleep as usual.

But then, Emily said some magic words ...

Bagpuss, dear Bagpuss,
Old fat furry cat-puss,
Wake up and look at this thing
that I bring.
Wake up, be bright,
Be golden and light!
Bagpuss! Oh hear what I sing!

Yawnnn!

And Bagpuss was wide awake and full of life and magic.

And when Bagpuss wakes up, all his friends wake up too.

The mice on the mouse organ woke up
and stretched.

Madeleine the rag doll woke up ...

So did Gabriel, the toad with the banjo

... and last of all,
Professor Yaffle, who is
a very distinguished
old woodpecker.

He climbed down off his bookend and went
to see what it was that Emily had brought.
I wonder what it was ...

Ship in a Bottle

"It's a dirty old bottle!" cried Yaffle. "That is nothing but a dirty old bottle! What on earth is the use of a dirty old bottle? It's so dirty I can't even see what's inside it!"

"Wait a minute! Wait a minute! We will do it!" shouted the mice as they ran to fetch their mops and buckets.

"We will wash it, we will splosh it,
Bring the bucket and mop mop mop,
We will dust it, we will brush it
We will polish its top top top."

sang the mice as they scrubbed and polished the bottle until it shone.

Then Professor Yaffle could see what was inside it.

"Bits of wood!" said Professor Yaffle, "broken bits of wood and cloth and pieces of string. I don't know why those things are in the bottle."

So the only thing to do was to go into the bottle and fetch the things out. The neck of the bottle was a bit small for Charliemouse to climb in but the other mice did their best to help.

"Push! Push! Push! Push!" they shouted.

"Stop!" shouted Madeleine. "You are hurting poor Charliemouse. Take him out at once!"

"Pull! Pull! Pull! Pull! ... POP!"

Out he came like a cork from a bottle.

"Listen," said Madeleine, "all you have to do is turn the bottle upside down, then the things will fall out."

"Of course! Yes! What a good idea! Come on mice!" they shouted as they took hold of the bottle.

"Heave! Heave! Heave!" they shouted as they lifted it.

This is what fell out of the bottle:

"Just as I said," muttered Professor Yaffle, "just broken bits of wood and scraps of cloth and string. Now I wonder what that can have been?"

Professor Yaffle looked very closely at the pieces from every side. Then he spoke: "Hmmm, hmmm, hmmm. That was a ship. That thing was once a ship in a bottle!"

Bagpuss was amazed.

"A ship?" he cried. "In a bottle? Where could it sail to? Who could sail in it? It would be much too small!"

"Too small for us!" squeaked the mice.

"Oh, I don't know," said Gabriel, "I once heard of a ship with mice for sailors ..."

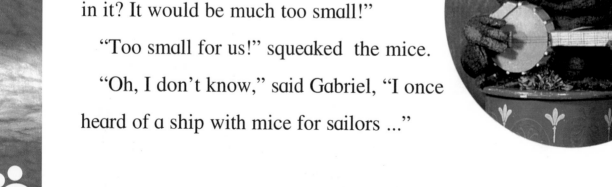

"Nerp, nerp, nerp," said Professor Yaffle sternly, "that's all very well but what we have to do is mend this poor broken ship! Bagpuss, what we need is a story. A proper magic story that will mend little broken ships. Please think for us, Bagpuss."

The mice fetched a sea captain's cap and put it on Bagpuss's head to help him think.

"Think for us Bagpuss!" they shouted. "Think for us Bagpuss, please!"

So Bagpuss thought.

He thought so hard that his thoughts appeared like magic above his head.

"Ah, yes, I remember," said Bagpuss, "I remember a story ... yes! Now be quiet and listen ..."

The Mermaid

"It all happened a long time ago," began Bagpuss,
"when I was a sea-captain and sailed the seven seas.
I steered my stout two-masted ship
before the western breeze.

One day the wind forgot to blow,
The sea was still, the day was fine.
Without a wind we could not go.
So I took out my rod and line
and settled down to fish.

(Well, yes, that's all there was to do, you see.
When the wind doesn't blow, the ship doesn't go.)

But I was Captain Bagpuss, I knew the thing to do.
I tied a pearl to the end of my line
And baited it with glue.

That way I caught a mermaid,
A pretty child was she.
She sat on my lap in the bo'sun's cap
And we all drank China tea.

We talked for a while and I said with a smile,
"May I ask you a favour dear please?
If I give you this pearl will you be a good girl
And send us a westerly breeze?"

"Delighted!" she cried and jumped over the side
And she dived with a flick of her tail.
But the breeze that she sent was not quite what we meant,
For she sent us a terrible gale.

Our poor ship was tossed and some pieces got lost,
And the wind blew away our best sail,
And then came a bump and a crash and a thump
Just as if we'd tripped over a whale.

It wasn't of course. It was something far worse.
We had hit this great island of rocks.
Our ship was all smashed and we were all dashed
On the shore without any dry socks.

The storm ended at last and the mermaid came past,
And she said she was ever so sorry,
But it wasn't too tragic, she'd do some more magic
And we would have no need to worry.

Then all of the mermaids for miles all around
Went diving and swimming until they had found
Every piece of our ship from the keel to the tip
And laid them all out in a heap on the ground.

Then the mermaids began a most beautiful song,
And the song they were singing was magic and strong.
The effect was unusual but true.

For the pieces of ship
'gan to jump and to skip
And soon they were dancing
And waltzing and prancing
And twirling and whirling
And squeaking and creaking
And stringing and ringing
And fitting together
In time with the measure,
Till when it was ended
The whole thing was mended
The ship was as perfect as new."

And so it was! The little ship had been perfectly mended by Bagpuss's magic story. All they had to do now was to put the ship back into the bottle.

"Too small! Too small!" said the mice, meaning the bottle.

"Too tall! Too tall!" said the mice, meaning the ship.

"Perfectly simple," said Professor Yaffle. "All tall ships in small bottles have folding masts. First of all, you must fold the masts flat. Then you push the ship very carefully into the bottle, and, very gently, pull on the cotton which is part of the rigging and that pulls up the masts and the sails.

Then, all you need is a dab of glue on the cotton to hold it in place and the job is done!"

The mice dipped Charliemouse's tail in the glue and he reached it in to glue the cotton. Then they pushed in the cork and the job was done.

There was the ship in the bottle as good as new!

All you ever wanted to know about ...
Bagpuss

FULL NAME
Bagpuss

AGE
As old as he feels

BIRTHPLACE
Katarpurr,
Northern India

CURRENT ADDRESS
The cushion in Emily's shop

BEST FRIENDS
Everybody

LIKES
A lovely sleep but will always be interested in a really good story!

DISLIKES
Having to stay awake too long!

FAVOURITE COLOUR
Pink stripes

FAVOURITE FOOD
Chocolate biscuits!

Find the Bottle

The mice want to put the mended ship back in the bottle but they can't find it.

Can **you** help them find their way to the bottle?

FINISH

The Mouse Mill

One day, Emily found a thing.

"It's a box," said Professor Yaffle.

"A box of what, I wonder."

"That's not a box," said Gabriel the toad. "That," he said firmly, "is a house."

"A house?" laughed Professor Yaffle. "No, that's a box!"

"That is a mouse house!" squeaked the mice from the mouse organ. "But it is not open yet. Wait a minute and we will do it!"

The mice hurried over to the box, and opened it up. They sang as they worked:

"We will bend it, we'll extend it
We will open up its top top top.
We will grow it, then we'll show it
This is what we've got got got!"

Then everyone could see that the box was a strange kind of house – with doors, windows, and some sort of crane.

"There's a wheel on the side of it, too," said Bagpuss. "How very peculiar. I wonder what kind of mouse would live in that sort of house."

"I know who lives in it!" piped up Charliemouse.

"Do you, Charliemouse?" said Bagpuss. "Well, you tell me."

"A miller," said Charliemouse, delighted.

"A miller!" said Bagpuss. "Of course! That is a mill and that is the mill wheel on the side."

"We'll ring the bell!" squeaked the mice, pulling a string.

CLANGGG rang an important-sounding bell. The front door opened with a creak and there stood ...

"Charliemouse!" said the mice. "Hallo, Charliemouse!"

"Hallo," said Charliemouse, who was dressed as a miller in an apron and cap.

"Nerp, nerp, nerp," crowed Professor Yaffle. "Do be serious. We're trying to find out what that thing is for."

"It's a mouse mill!" said Charliemouse.

"A mouse mill?" said Bagpuss. "What does it make?"

"Chocolate biscuits!" said Charliemouse, proudly.

"Fiddlesticks and flapdoodle!" said Professor Yaffle, rattling his wooden woodpecker wings. "There's no such thing as a mill that makes chocolate biscuits."

"What does it make the chocolate biscuits out of?" Bagpuss asked.

"Breadcrumbs and butterbeans," said Charliemouse, firmly.

"Ridiculous!" said Professor Yaffle. "You can't make chocolate biscuits out of breadcrumbs and butterbeans."

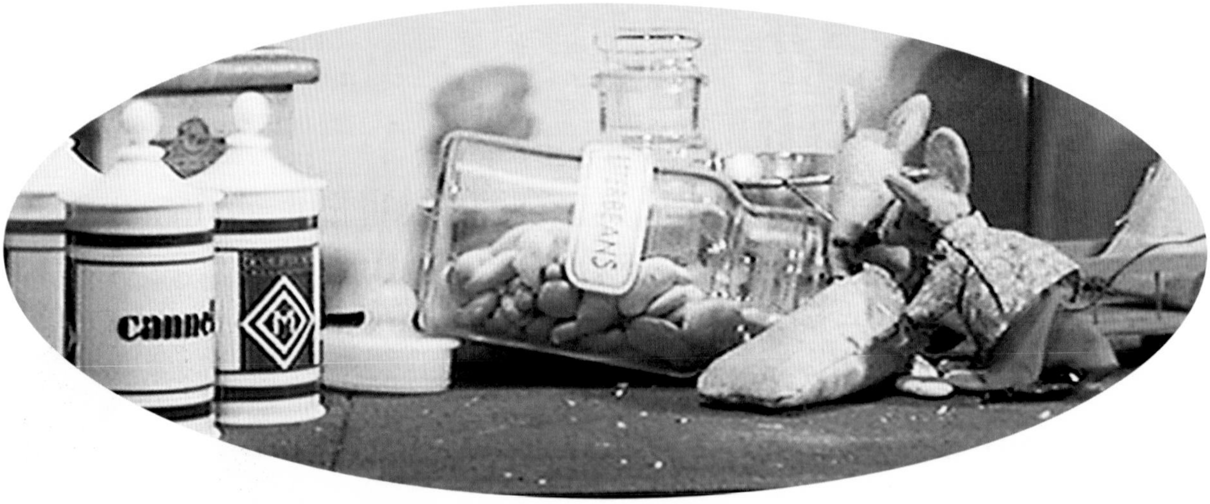

The mice set about proving that they could do just that. Gabriel the toad played some magic chocolate-biscuit-making music on his banjo, while the mice rushed about gathering breadcrumbs and butterbeans from the kitchen shelves.

"Breadcrumbs first, please," said Charliemouse. The mice hoisted a bag of breadcrumbs up into the mill.

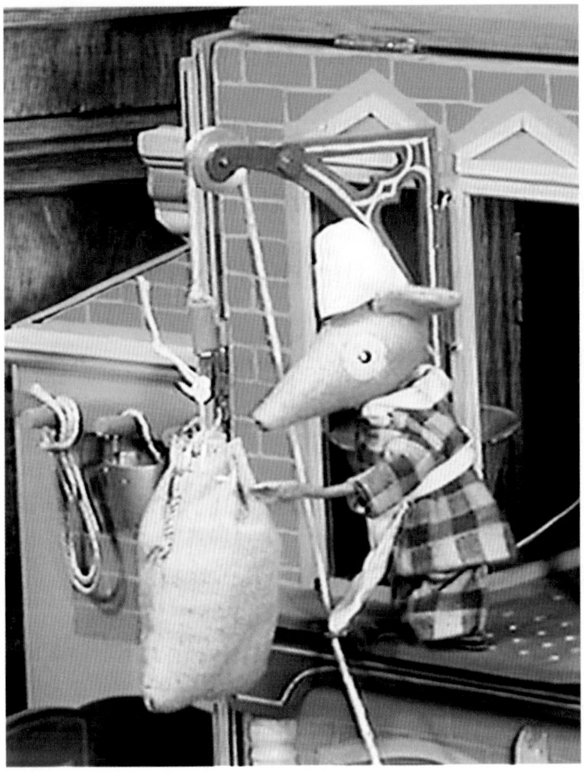

“Heave! Heave! Heave!” Charliemouse emptied the bag of breadcrumbs into the mill. “Now the butterbeans,” he said. The mice hoisted the butterbeans up into the mill. The mill was now ready.

“The marvellous, mechanical mouse mill!” announced Charliemouse. A mouse wound the key and, with a splendid grating noise, wheels wound and grinders ground. Then a delivery chute opened up and a chocolate biscuit came tumbling out. A mouse took the biscuit away in a trolley.

Professor Yaffle felt quite dizzy watching the mill wheel going round and round ...

“Keep it going!” called out Charliemouse. The mice came running from behind the mill with sacks of breadcrumbs and butterbeans, which were hoisted up into the mill. A chocolate biscuit rattled out the chute and was whisked away.

"Real chocolate biscuits!" said Bagpuss. "The mice put the breadcrumbs and butterbeans in the top, they work the mill and out come chocolate biscuits."

"It's impossible!" said Professor Yaffle. "I'm going round the back to see what is happening."

"No Yaffles round the back!" said the Mice, trying to stop Professor Yaffle. But Professor Yaffle was stronger than the mice.

"Stop the mill!" commanded Professor Yaffle, examining the back of the mill. "Now then. That's the place where the breadcrumbs go in and that leads down to the breadcrumb bag. And that's the place where the butterbeans go in and that leads down to the butterbean bag. Then I suppose you mice wheel the bags round to the front and hoist them up again."

"That's right," chorused the mice. "That's what we do."

"So what makes the chocolate biscuits?" asked Professor Yaffle.

"We send a chocolate biscuit down the chute," said a mouse, "the chocolate biscuit is delivered to the trolley and Williemouse brings it back again."

"So you use the same chocolate biscuit over and over again!" flapped Professor Yaffle.

"That's right!" said the mice.

"So, it's all a trick!" cried Professor Yaffle. "You don't make chocolate biscuits out of breadcrumbs and butterbeans!"

"Of course not!" laughed the mice. "You can't make chocolate biscuits that way!"

"It was a rotten trick!" said Professor Yaffle, crossly.

"I did sort of suspect it was a trick," said Bagpuss.

"Push the mill into the window," said Madeleine. "So that the person who has lost it might see it."

"Heave! Heave! Heave!" said the mice, as they pushed the mouse mill into the window.

"It was a good trick, though wasn't it?" yawned Bagpuss.

All you ever wanted to know about ...
The Mice

NAMES
Charlie, Lizzie, Willie, Tilly, Jenny, Eddie and Milly

AGES
"One, two, three, four, five ..."

BIRTHPLACE
The hole under the counter

CURRENT ADDRESS
The mouse organ, Emily's shop

BEST FRIENDS
Each other, and Bagpuss

LIKES
Singing and scrubbing

DISLIKES
Having nothing to do

FAVOURITE COLOUR
All sorts, preferably liquorice!

FAVOURITE FOOD
Smelly Stilton cheese

Catch the Mice!

Bagpuss can hear the mice singing but he can't see them!
Can you help Bagpuss find all the mice?
There are seven to catch!

ANSWERS Mouse 1 is peeping out from behind the drawers. Mouse 2 is standing on the top shelf. Mouse 3 is crouching on the sideboard. Mouse 4 is holding onto Bagpuss's fur. Mouse 5 is sitting on Bagpuss's cushion. Mouse 6 is holding on to Bagpuss's tail. Mouse 7 is hiding on the floor.

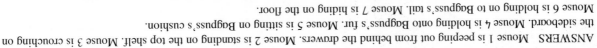

Bagpuss

Competition Time

We've got some beautiful Bagpuss soft toys, courtesy of Golden Bear. Carefully created and designed to bring Bagpuss to life, Golden Bear products are of the highest standards. Children love them, parents trust them. These beautiful soft toys are authentic in every detail.

First Prize

A big, cuddly Bagpuss Backpack.

Second Prize

A yawning Bagpuss.

Plus 15 Bagpuss Beanie Toys for runners up.

HOW TO ENTER

All you have to do is unscramble these letters to spell out the name of a close friend of Bagpuss:

BAGLIRE

Write your answer on a postcard or on the back of a sealed envelope (don't forget to put your name, address and age) and post it to:

BAGPUSS ANNUAL COMPETITION,
EGMONT WORLD LIMITED, DEANWAY TECHNOLOGY CENTRE,
WILMSLOW ROAD, HANDFORTH, CHESHIRE SK9 3FB

RULES

1. 17 winners will be chosen at random and notified by post.
2. Judges' decision will be final. No correspondence will be entered into.
3. The winners' names will be made available from Egmont World Limited (on request) after 5th February 2001. Please enclose a stamped addressed envelope for reply.
4. Employees (and their relatives) of Egmont World Limited and their associated companies are not eligible to enter.
5. Entries are limited to one per person.
6. Competition is open to residents of the UK, Channel Islands, and Ireland only.
7. The Publishers reserve the right to vary prizes, subject to availability.
8. Closing date for entries is 26th January 2001.

Spot the Difference!

It's Christmas time in Emily's Shop but something is not quite right!

Can you find the differences between these two festive scenes. There are ten differences to find.

ANSWERS: 1. A loop of paper chain has appeared. 2. A vase of feathers has appeared. 3. Gabriel is back on his drum.
4. The picture of Emily has disappeared from the wall. 5. Madeleine is holding a red present instead of a blue one.
6. One of the mice has disappeared from the mouse organ. 7. Presents have disappeared from beside the mouse organ.
8. Bagpuss's hat has changed to green. 9. A stick of candy has appeared at the bottom of the tree. 10. Two crackers have disappeared.

The Owls Of Athens

One day, Emily found a thing.

"That is a very musty old, crusty old, piece of rag," said Professor Yaffle scornfully. "It is much too old and dirty for us to see what it is."

"Wait!" shouted the mice. "We will wash it!" They sang as they went to fetch mops and scrubbing brushes:

"We will rub it, we will scrub it
We will wash it and a rub-a-dub.
We will soak it, we will soap it
We will boil it in our tin tub!"

"Stop! Stop!" shouted Madeleine. "That is a very delicate piece of fabric. If you go bashing and scrubbing at it, you will spoil it forever! You must treat it gently, lovingly and very politely. Now, one mouse may very gently brush one part of the cloth with one soft brush."

Williemouse came forward and brushed very carefully. "Brush, brush, brush," said Williemouse. Slowly, slowly, a pattern began to appear. Or was it a picture?

"A wowl! A wowl!" shrieked the mice. They fled and hid behind the mouse organ. Something had frightened them.

What was it?

"It's a picture of an owl," said Professor Yaffle as he examined the cloth. "That's all it is. It's a very old picture of an owl and it has ancient Greek writing on it ... 'A', 'TH', 'E', which means Athens. That is Obol, the owl of Athens – and if you remember that then you will really know something!"

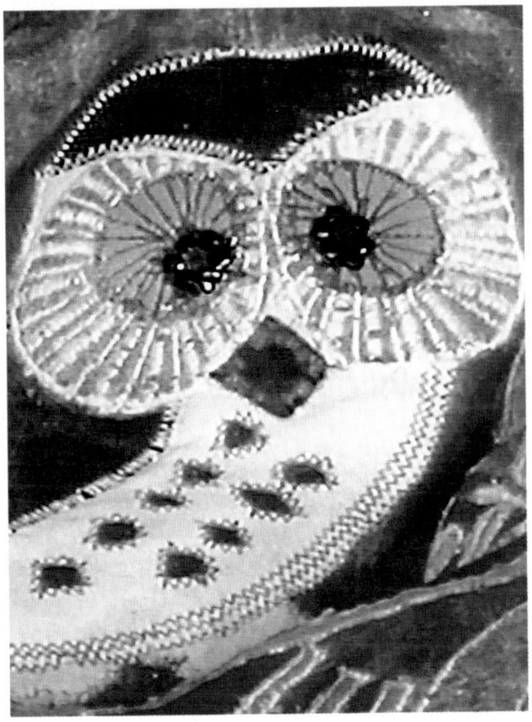

"The Owls of Athens," said Madeleine. "Yes! They were kings among birds and famous for their beautiful singing."

"Stuff and nonsense!" crowed Professor Yaffle. "Owls don't sing! They make a sort of hooting noise. You know, to wit, to woo, or words to that effect."

"Maybe you are right," nodded Madeleine, "But I know an ancient story about the Owls of Athens."

"Well, tell it to us then!" said Professor Yaffle.

"Come out from behind the organ, mice," said Madeleine. "Turn the page and I will tell you the story of The Owls of Athens ..."

"At night, in the groves of olive trees that grew on the mountainsides above the city of Athens in Ancient Greece, the owls would gather together and sing lovely songs in the moonlight.

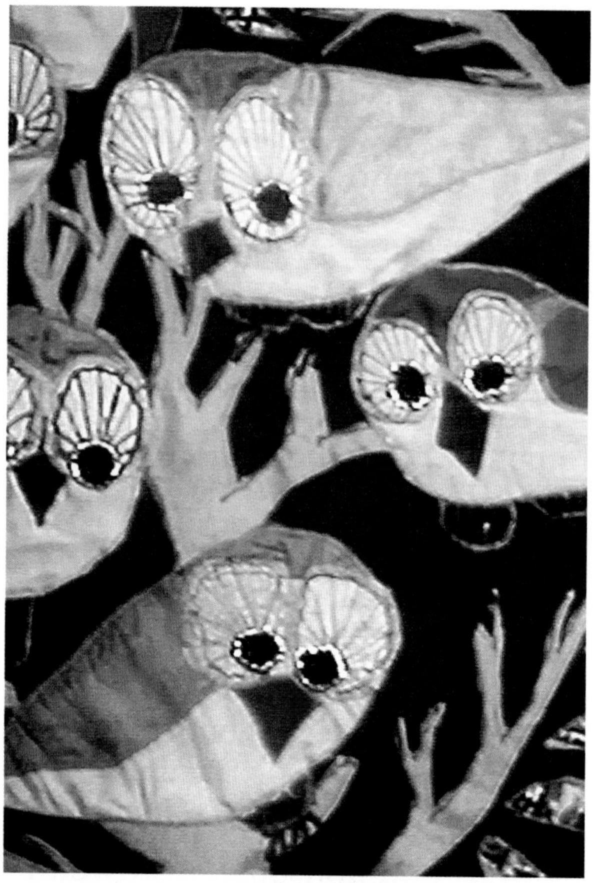

The owls of Athens sang so beautifully and sweetly that all the animals would come to listen.

This pleased the owls enormously. They said to each other, "Surely we are kings and queens and should be treated as kings and queens."

So the owls told the animals that they would only sing to them if they brought presents; not just good things to eat but gold and silver and jewels. Well, the animals loved to hear the owls sing and so, as they had no gold or silver of their own, they crept into the houses of people and stole gold and silver and jewels and took them to the owls.

This pleased the owls very much indeed and they sang, "Now we are truly the kings and queens of all!" And they sang most sweetly together that night, and the next night, and the night after.

And each night the pile of glittering treasure grew larger and larger, until one night – one clear, cloudless night – the moon passing overhead saw the pile of treasure glittering in her light.

Then the moon spoke to the owls. She said, “Oh, owls! Where did you learn to sing so sweetly?”

The owls replied, “Oh, moon! We did not need to learn. We were born able to sing so sweetly. Are we not kings and queens among birds?”

Then the moon said, “Why do the animals bring you glittering treasure?” The owls replied, “Oh, moon, they bring us treasure because we told them that if they didn’t we would not sing to them. Are we not the cleverest of all birds?”

The moon did not answer. She sailed away through the sky on her journey. But as she went, she spoke one word of magic. At once, there came into the world a number of small, brown, ordinary-looking birds. At least, they looked ordinary. But the moon called them nightingales and perched them in the very tops of the trees.

The next night, the owls sang together as usual. But no animals came to hear them, nobody brought them treasure. They sang alone in the empty grove.

An owl said, "Why has nobody come to hear us sing?" Another owl said, "Listen!" All around them, in the tops of trees, the nightingales were singing.

As they listened, the owls knew that the singing of the nightingales was far sweeter than the singing of owls. They knew that nobody would ever come to hear them again and bring them gold and silver and jewels.

The owls were angry. They were furious. Who could have played such a trick on them?

"Who? Who? Who?" said the owls. Then they saw the moon smiling.

"You! Moon, you! You are who!" they hooted.

"That is the sort of song for owls to sing!" laughed the moon. "And that shall be their song!"

And so, from that day to this, that has been the song of the owls.

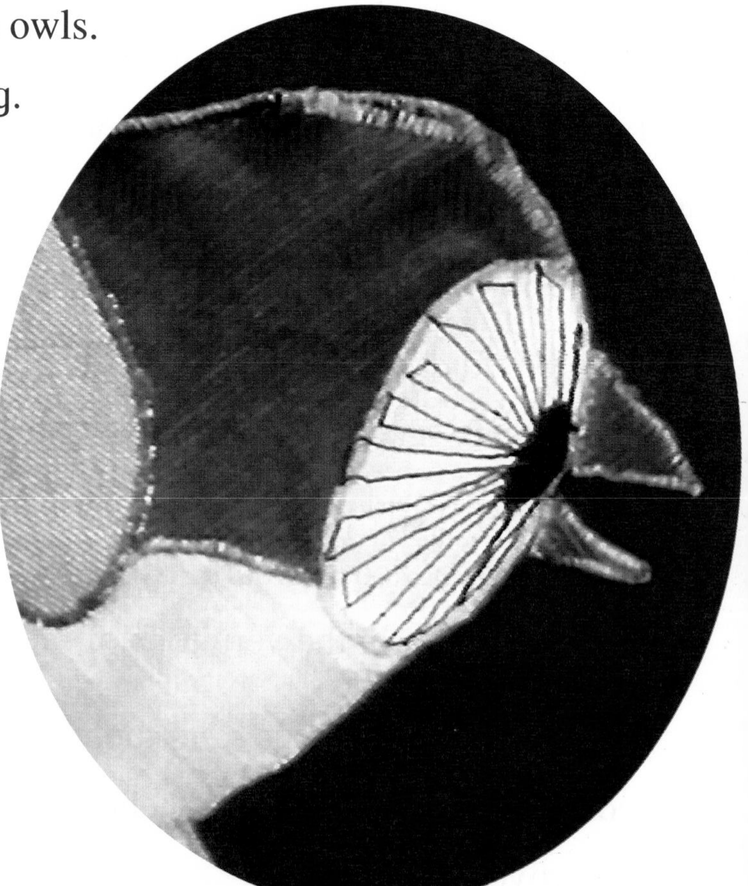

"That was a very proper story," said Professor Yaffle approvingly. "Those owls were proud and greedy."

"I think it was a sad story," said Madeleine. "Poor owls."

"You can see all the story in the pattern on the cloth," said Bagpuss, looking at the piece of old rag. Only it wasn't a piece of old rag any more.

"That is a cushion cover," said Professor Yaffle. "The cover of a cushion for a king."

"The cover of a cushion for a king," repeated Bagpuss. "He must have been a very small king."

"He was very small," said Gabriel. "Very bony and cold too in places!"

"I know!" said Madeleine. "The Bony King of Nowhere! Come on, let's sing it!"

"Wait for us!" chorused the mice, jumping on to the mouse organ. "Heave! Heave! Heave!" They heaved the roll of music into the slot and began to pump the bellows. The marvellous mechanical mouse organ sighed and groaned and puffed and started to play ...

The Bony King of Nowhere

The bony king of Nowhere
He sat upon his throne.
He didn't much like sitting there
Because his throne was * * * *
His throne was made of stone.

His throne was made of marble white
Its feet were made of gold
It was a royal throne all right
But, oh dear! It was * * * *
It was extremely cold.

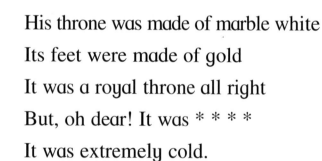

He jumped up on the tea table
And said, "Please will you find
A seat that's soft and suitable
To warm a king's be- * * * *
Just to see what you can find!"

They fetched him up a hammock
But they couldn't keep it still
They put him on a rocking-horse,
The rocking made him * * * *
It made him feel quite ill!

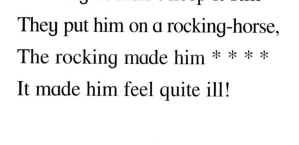

They sat him on a woolsack
But that rubbed up his knees.
They rolled him on a feather-bed
But that just made him * * * *
It simply made him sneeze!

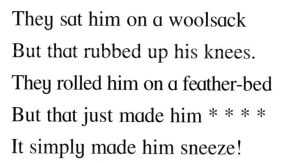

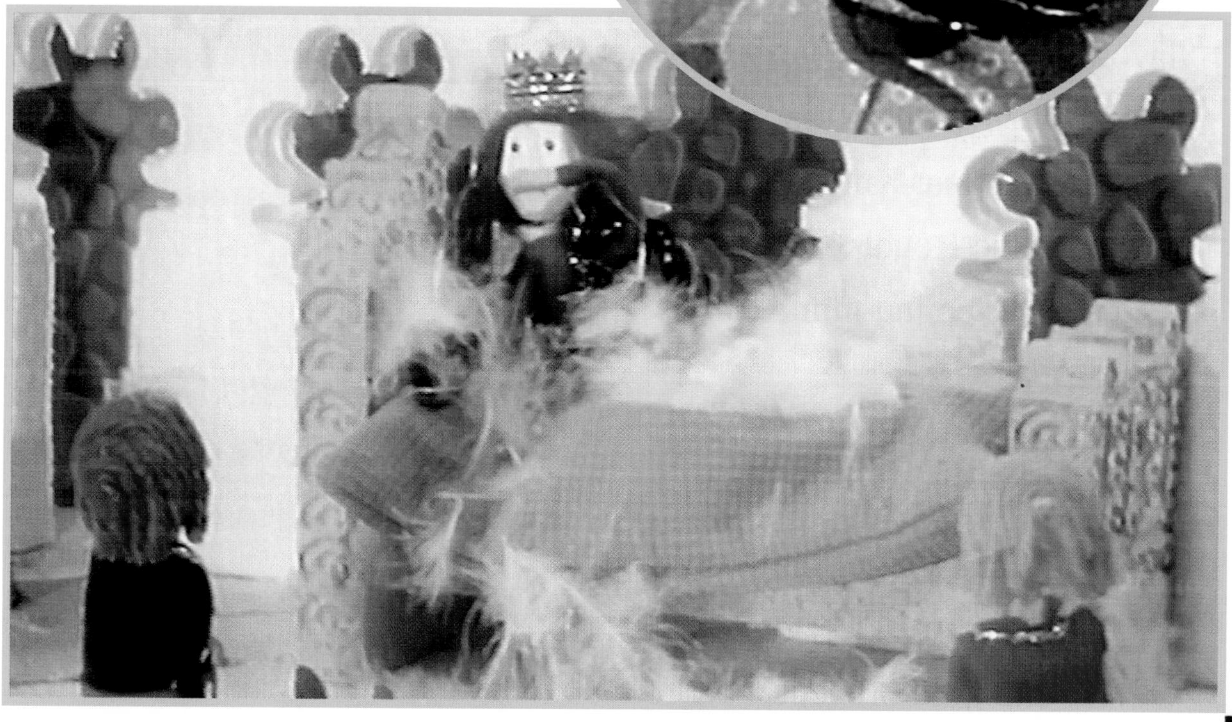

That poor old king of Nowhere
Just sat there looking sad
He said, "If you could help me
I'd be very very * * * *
Particularly glad!"

Two mice came up from somewhere
Behind their royal chum.
They said, "Dear King, here is a thing,
To warm the Royal * * *
And stop it feeling numb."

The thing it was a cushion bright
Of silk and gold brocade.
So square and soft and small and light
And very neatly * * * *
Of silk and gold brocade.

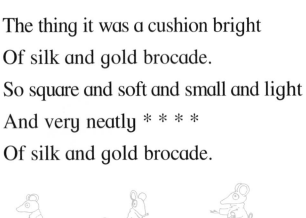

Now the happy king of Nowhere
Is smiling on his throne,
His smile is rosy, his seat is cosy,
Although his throne is stone, is stone.
The mice have made it nice, so nice,
He is a happy king!

"Look!" squealed the mice. "We have mended the cushion!" They had edged it with gold braid and filled it with cotton wool. It looked as good as new. "It is a cushion fit for a king!" they cried. "All we need now is a king!"

Bagpuss coughed modestly.

"Well, it is a cushion fit for a king," he said, "but as we do not have a king, I might just mention that it is a cushion fit for a cat."

"Certainly not," snapped Yaffle. "Cushions for kings are not cushions for cats."

Bagpuss looked so disappointed that the mice fetched gold paper and scissors and glue and made him a rather crooked paper crown.

"Now you are a king," they said. "The fat-cat king of somewhere." Bagpuss smiled happily and settled down on the cushion.

"Delicious, sumptuous, exquisitely luxurious," sighed Bagpuss.

All you ever wanted to know about ...

Professor Yaffle

FULL NAME
Augustus Barclay Yaffle

AGE
Won't tell!

BIRTHPLACE
Carved from an old tree.

CURRENT ADDRESS
The bookend, Emily's shop.

BEST FRIENDS
Mainly Yaffle and Madeleine but he is in love with a clockwork ballerina

LIKES
Things to be right

DISLIKES
Foolishness and Flapdoodle!

FAVOURITE COLOUR
Brown

FAVOURITE FOOD
Toasted sawdust

What a Noise!

Here are some words which sound like other words.
Read the clues and look at the pictures.
Then fill in the squares on the opposite page.

1. This spoke one word of magic.
   Sounds like ...

2. The moon played this on the owls.
   Sounds like ...

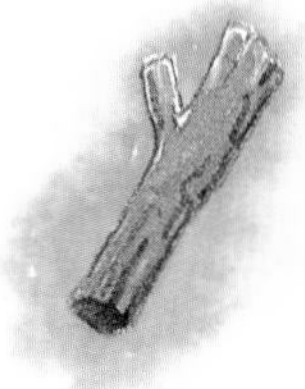

3. The owls wanted to be treated as queens and?
   Sounds like ...

4. Now, all owls make this sound.
   Sounds like ...

5. The nightingales perched in one of these.
   Sounds like ...

1

2

3

4

5

Now read downwards to find out when the owls sing!

ANSWERS 1. moon 2. trick 3. kings 4. hoot 5. tree
Word going down - night.

All you ever wanted to know about ...

Madeleine

FULL NAME
Madeleine Remnant

AGE
Never ask a lady her age!

BIRTHPLACE
Granny's rag-bag

CURRENT ADDRESS
The wicker chair, Emily's shop

BEST FRIENDS
All the mice, and Bagpuss of course!

LIKES
Singing and telling stories

DISLIKES
Things being hurt

FAVOURITE COLOUR
Mouse grey

FAVOURITE FOOD
Custard creams

All you ever wanted to know about ...

Gabriel

FULL NAME
Gabriel Croaker
(of the "Tea-Time toads")

AGE
Two as a tadpole,
Ten as a toad

BIRTHPLACE
In the Musical Box on
the Telly

CURRENT ADDRESS
On top of the round tin,
Emily's shop

BEST FRIENDS
Madeleine

LIKES
Remembering songs

DISLIKES
Getting too dry

FAVOURITE COLOUR
Slime-green

FAVOURITE FOOD
Wet jelly babies

Happy Christmas!

Look! Bagpuss and all his friends have made a lovely Christmas card for Emily.
It has lots of things in the picture.
What can you see?

Christmas pudding

red present

piece of holly

gold star

jingle bell

Santa's hat

red berries

Christmas crackers

little Charliemouse

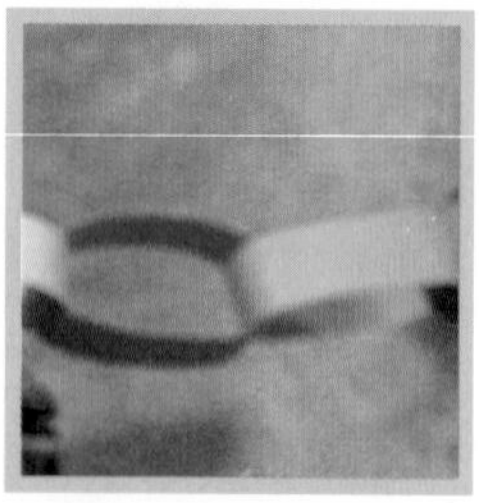
paper chains

Santa Bagpuss

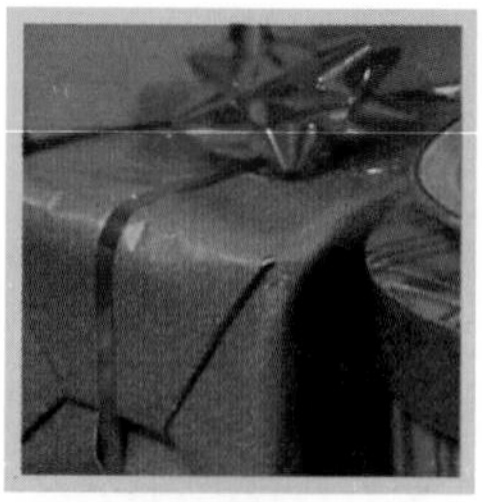
gold present

Who lives where?

Before Bagpuss goes to sleep, everyone in Emily's shop has to be in their own special place.
Look at the pictures below.
Can you match each character to its special place?

1

2

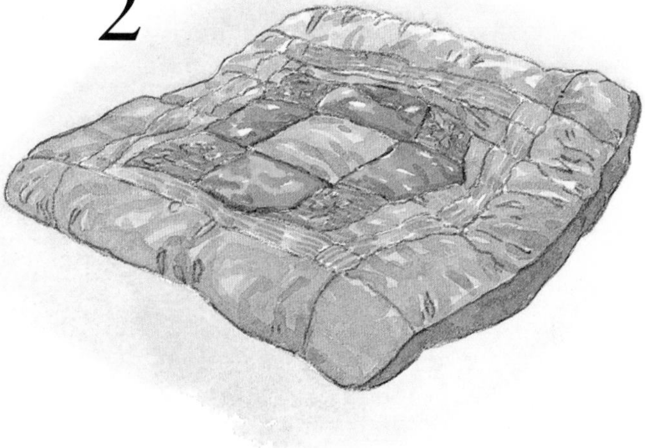

3

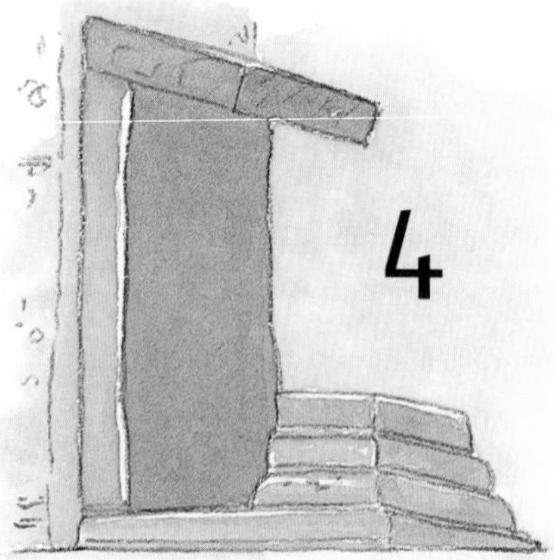

4

5

6

7

8

9

10

ANSWERS Professor Yaffle (1) with bookend (4). Bagpuss (3) with cushion (2). Gabriel (5) with drum (10). Mice (8) with mouse organ (6). Madeleine (9) with chair (7).

Bagpuss gave a big yawn and settled down to sleep, and of course, when Bagpuss goes to sleep ...

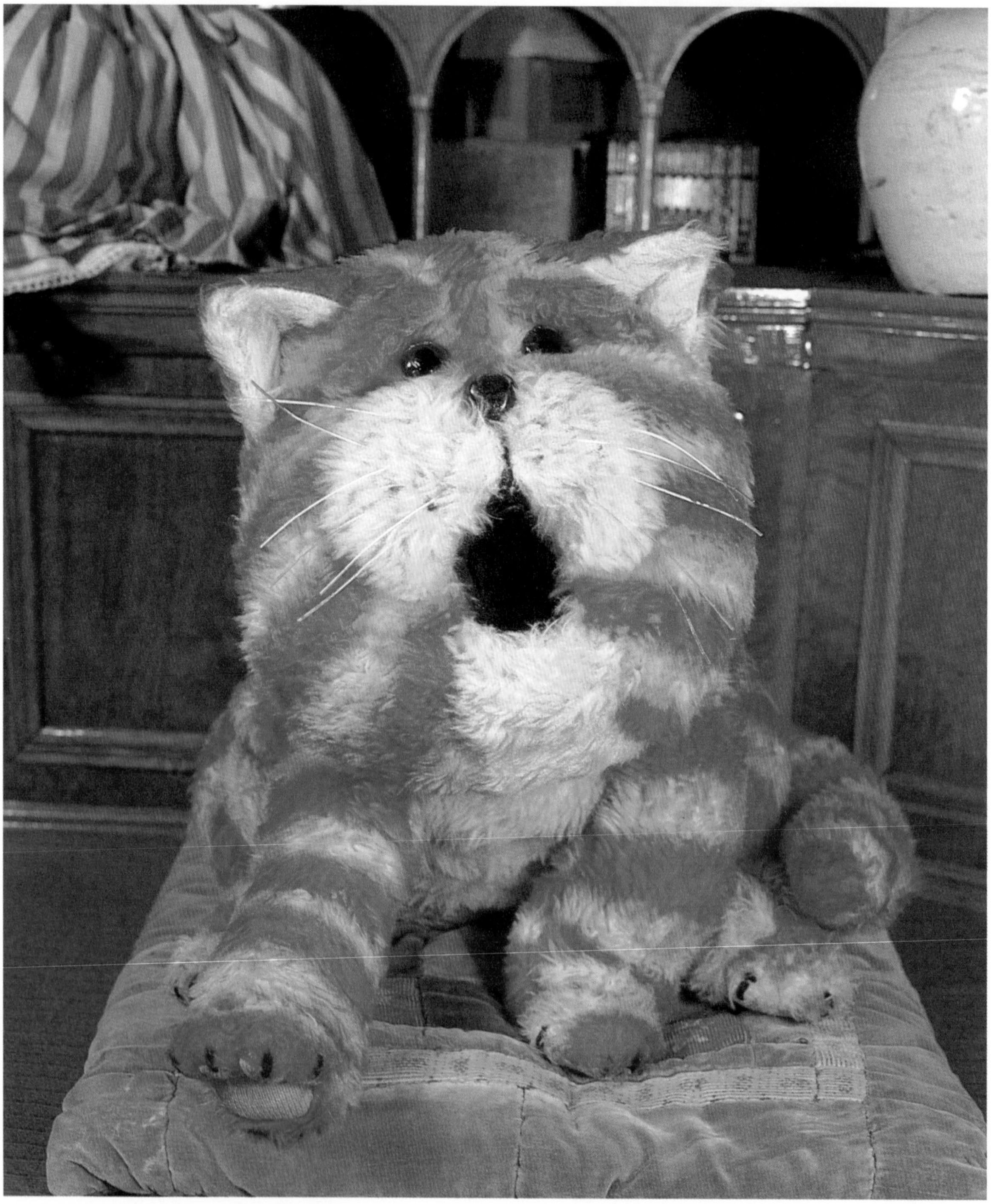

all his friends go to sleep too.

The mice were ornaments on the mouse organ.

Gabriel and Madeleine were just dolls.

And Professor Yaffle was just a carved wooden bookend in the shape of a woodpecker.

Even Bagpuss himself, once he was asleep, was just an old saggy cloth cat, baggy and a bit loose at the seams.

But Emily loved him.